Who'll Mind Henry?

Who'll Mind

Henry?

By Anne Mallett

Illustrated by Sheila Greenwald

DOUBLEDAY & COMPANY, INC.   GARDEN CITY, NEW YORK

Mallett

Library of Congress Catalog Card Number 65-17776
Text copyright © 1965 by Anne Mallett
Illustrations copyright © 1965 by Sheila Greenwald
All Rights Reserved
Printed in the United States of America
First Edition

8

It was a lovely day.

Mrs. Morse stood on the front porch reading her shopping list: a new softball for David, ice cream for Henry, shoelaces, blue thread, birdseed, return the borrowed cake pan to Mrs. Burns, and then go to the dentist.

"David, take good care of Henry," she said. "I will be back as soon as I possibly can." And she started off toward Mrs. Burns's house to return the cake pan.

David liked Henry. Sometimes he even liked taking care of Henry. But today he had a feeling there was something he should be doing that he had forgotten about.

Just then a truck stopped in front of the house and dumped a large bundle of newspapers on the sidewalk.

"Of course!" cried David. "This is Friday, and I have to deliver the weekly newspaper. But who will take care of Henry?"

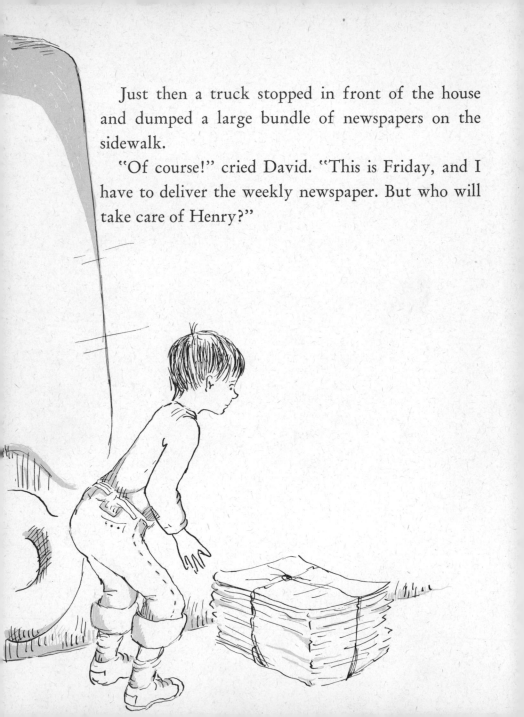

Mr. Roberts, the mailman, heard him.

"Hello, David," he said. "I'll be glad to take care of Henry for a while. I'll just put him in my mailbag. He's kind of big for three, but I think I can squeeze him in."

"Oh boy!" cried Henry.

In no time at all, David was off on his bike delivering papers, and Henry was going from house to house in Mr. Roberts' mailbag.

It was like being a papoose in a cradleboard, and Henry liked it.

On every front porch Mr. Roberts turned around and backed up so Henry could ring the doorbell two times.

It was a lovely day.

Looking out of Mrs. Burns's window, Mrs. Morse exclaimed, "Why, that looks like Henry in Mr. Roberts' mailbag. But it *couldn't* be, of course. He's at home with David."

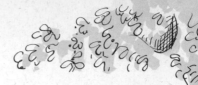

When they got to the end of the street, Mr. Roberts opened the big mailbox. And when he saw how many letters there were, he realized that there wouldn't be room for Henry in his mailbag any more. "Who will take care of Henry now?" he wondered.

"Hi there, Mr. Roberts. Hello, Henry," called the ice-cream man. "Henry, how would you like to have the ride in my truck that I've been promising you?"

"Oh, yes, Mr. Wilson!" cried Henry.

"You came at just the right time," said Mr. Roberts. "David should be back soon, but I can't wait for him because of all this mail that must be delivered."

Henry happily climbed into the truck and started to ring the bell with all his might. Mr. Wilson gave him a large chocolate ice-cream cone and put his special hat on Henry's head.

Passing by on his bike, David thought, "GEE, that looks like Henry." There were so many children around the truck that he really couldn't see. "But of course, it *couldn't* be," he said to himself, and he kept on riding.

And Henry kept on ringing the bell. With so many customers, Mr. Wilson was soon sold out.

Mr. Wilson had to leave Henry with Mr. White at the gas station while he went to get more ice cream for his truck.

"You can hold my wrenches for me, Henry," said Mr. White.

When David stopped by the gas station to put air in his bicycle tires, he saw two pairs of feet sticking out from under a red truck. Two of the feet were enormous and had huge brown boots on them. The other feet were small and wore sneakers spotted with paint.

"That's funny," David thought. "Those sneakers sure look like Henry's." But knowing Henry was with the mailman, David kept on riding.

And Henry kept on assisting Mr. White.

Henry liked repairing cars, and he particularly liked the thick black gooey stuff he found underneath the truck.

"Oh-oh, that's grease," cried Mr. White, "and there is nearly as much on you as there is on the car. Maybe the Smiths' toy store would be a better place for you to play until David comes to take you home."

25

Mrs. Smith was very glad to see Henry again. "I still have that yellow duck you like so much," she told Henry. "You can play with it this morning."

Henry's mother just happened to glance in the toy store window as she passed by on her way to the dentist.

"Goodness, that looks like Henry," she thought. But the chocolate ice cream on his cheek, and the spots of grease all over him were a good disguise. And besides, the yellow duck in his arms hid much of his face.

So Henry's mother just shook her head and kept on walking.

And Henry kept on playing.

For a long time he was very happy playing, but finally he put both arms around the duck, and his cheek on the duck's soft head, and closed his eyes.

"Why, Henry is going to sleep," whispered Mrs. Smith. "I have no comfortable place for a boy to take a nap here. I wonder if Mr. Barton has sold that crib in his store window."

So she picked up Henry, duck and all, and carried
him to the furniture store next door.

Henry settled down in the crib with his duck. Sleepily he watched the people walking by on the sidewalk. He tried to wave whenever he saw someone he knew, but finally it was too much trouble, and he fell asleep.

Mr. Barton was very glad to let Henry sleep in his crib. "A crib always looks nicer with a child in it," he said.

He was sound asleep when David went by on his
bike.

"Funny, that looked just like Henry. But I know
it *couldn't* be," thought David, so he kept on riding.
And Henry kept on sleeping.

Half an hour later Mrs. Warren walked into the
store, pulling her twins in a wagon.

"We need a new crib, Mr. Barton," she said.

Mr. Barton was delighted to make the sale, until
he thought about Henry, sound asleep in that very
crib.

"One more child won't make any difference," said Mrs. Warren. "I'm on my way to the fire station with Mr. Warren's lunch. I'll take Henry with me and then I can take him home."

Mrs. Warren put Henry between the twins in the wagon, and off they all went.

Mrs. Morse sat straight up in the dentist's chair and peered out the window. "That child looks just like Henry!" she exclaimed. "But of course, it *couldn't* be."

So she leaned back in the chair and the dentist went right on cleaning her teeth.

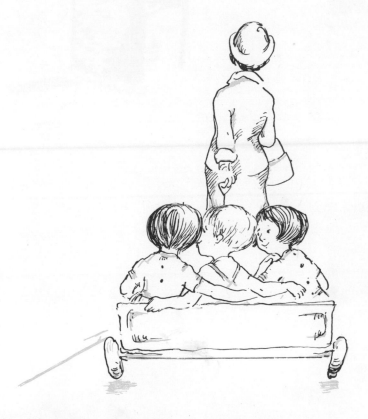

And Mrs. Warren went right on taking Henry to the fire station.

Henry liked the twins very much, and he just loved the fire station. Mr. Warren let them slide down the pole as long as he was standing down below to catch them.

Henry was having so much fun he didn't want to leave when Mrs. Warren had to go home.

"Leave him with us," said all the firemen. "Henry is no trouble at all. We'll let him play a while longer, and then one of the men will take him home."

Everything was fine until suddenly there was a shrill fire alarm. All the firemen leaped to their posts. Then they cried, "What will we do with Henry? We can't take him to the fire!"

Officer Kelly drove by the station when he heard the alarm. "Better let me take Henry home in my police car," he said. "You will be much too busy to watch out for him."

The fire engines raced down the streets of the town. The sirens wailed, and all traffic stopped. People gathered on the sidewalk to watch, and among them was Mrs. Morse.

47

As the police car sped by, she thought she saw a small familiar figure sitting beside Mr. Kelly.

"It just *couldn't* be Henry," she cried.

David had finished delivering his papers and was taking a short cut home, when he had to pull his bike way over to the side of the road to let the fire engines and the police car go by.

"Gee! No! It *couldn't* be Henry!" thought David, and on he rode.

David got home just as his mother came walking
briskly along the sidewalk.

And at that very moment, Officer Kelly drove up,
and helped Henry out of the police car.

David and his mother looked at Henry.

They saw the glob of chocolate ice cream on his cheek, the grease on his pants, and the large yellow duck in his arms.

Then they looked at each other.

Then they looked at Henry again.

Henry just smiled a great big happy smile. It had been *such* a lovely day.

EVERYONE had taken care of Henry!